my itty-bitty bio

Kobe Bryant

Published in the United States of America by Cherry Lake Publishing Group
Ann Arbor, Michigan
www.cherrylakepublishing.com

Reading Adviser: Beth Walker Gambro, MS, Ed., Reading Consultant, Yorkville, IL
Book Designer: Jennifer Wahi
Illustrator: Jeff Bane

Photo Credits: ©Cenz07/Shutterstock, 5; © Pal2iyawit/Shutterstock, 7; © Jerry Coli/Dreamstime, 9, 22; © Gene Wang/flickr, 11; © Featureflash Photo Agency, 13; © Stephaniemeiling/Dreamstime, 15, 23; © Photo Works/Shutterstock, 17; © Marie Elena Sager/Dreamstime, 19; ©_bukley/Shutterstock, 21; Cover, 1, 6, 8, 14, Jeff Bane; Various frames throughout, Shutterstock

Copyright ©2022 by Cherry Lake Publishing Group
All rights reserved. No part of this book may be reproduced or utilized in any form or by any means without written permission from the publisher.

Cherry Lake Press is an imprint of Cherry Lake Publishing Group.

Library of Congress Cataloging-in-Publication Data

Names: Fisher, Erin, author. | Bane, Jeff, 1957- illustrator.
Title: Kobe Bryant / by Erin Fisher ; illustrated by Jeff Bane.
Description: Ann Arbor, Michigan : Cherry Lake Publishing, 2021. | Series: My itty-bitty bio | Includes index.
Identifiers: LCCN 2021007980 (print) | LCCN 2021007981 (ebook) | ISBN 9781534186873 (hardcover) | ISBN 9781534188273 (paperback) | ISBN 9781534189676 (pdf) | ISBN 9781534191075 (ebook)
Subjects: LCSH: Bryant, Kobe, 1978-2020--Juvenile literature. | Basketball players--United States--Biography--Juvenile literature. | African American basketball players--Biography--Juvenile literature.
Classification: LCC GV884.B794 F57 2021 (print) | LCC GV884.B794 (ebook) | DDC 796.323092 [B]--dc23
LC record available at https://lccn.loc.gov/2021007980
LC ebook record available at https://lccn.loc.gov/2021007981

Printed in the United States of America
Corporate Graphics

table of contents

My Story 4

Timeline 22

Glossary 24

Index 24

About the illustrator: Jeff Bane and his two business partners own a studio along the American River in Folsom, California, home of the 1849 Gold Rush. When Jeff's not sketching or illustrating for clients, he's either swimming or kayaking in the river to relax.

my story

My name is Kobe Bryant.
I was born in Pennsylvania on
August 23, 1978.

My dad was a basketball player.

I knew I wanted to play too.

I spent 20 years playing basketball for the Lakers. They are a team in Los Angeles, California.

We won five **NBA championships**.

What is your favorite NBA team?

I was one of the best players.
I was a fan favorite.

People thought I wanted to be like Michael Jordan.

I just wanted to be myself.

Who is someone you want to be like?

I won many awards.

I won two **Olympic** gold medals.

I was known as the "**Black Mamba**."

I died in an accident in 2020. My daughter was with me.

The world was shocked. Many people were sad.

But my **legacy** remains. I was one of the greatest basketball players.

My family continues to **honor** my memory. So do my fans and teammates.

What would you like to ask me?

timeline

1996

1960

Born
1978

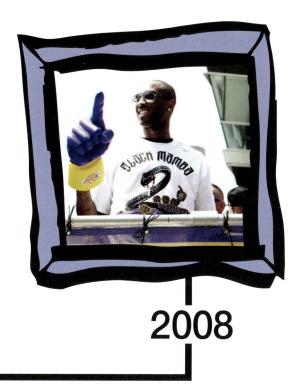

2008

2060

Died
2020

glossary

black mamba (BLAK MAHM-buh) a deadly snake

championships (CHAM-pee-uhn-ships) the final games in a sports series

honor (ON-ur) showing respect

legacy (LEG-uh-see) the achievements of a person's life

NBA (EN BEE AY) the National Basketball Association

Olympic (oh-LIM-pik) a part of the Olympics, an international sporting event

index

accident, 16
awards, 14

basketball, 6, 8, 18
Black Mamba, 14

fan, 10, 20

Jordan, Michael, 12

Lakers, 8
Los Angeles, California, 8

NBA, 8, 9

Olympic, 14

Pennsylvania, 4

teammates, 20